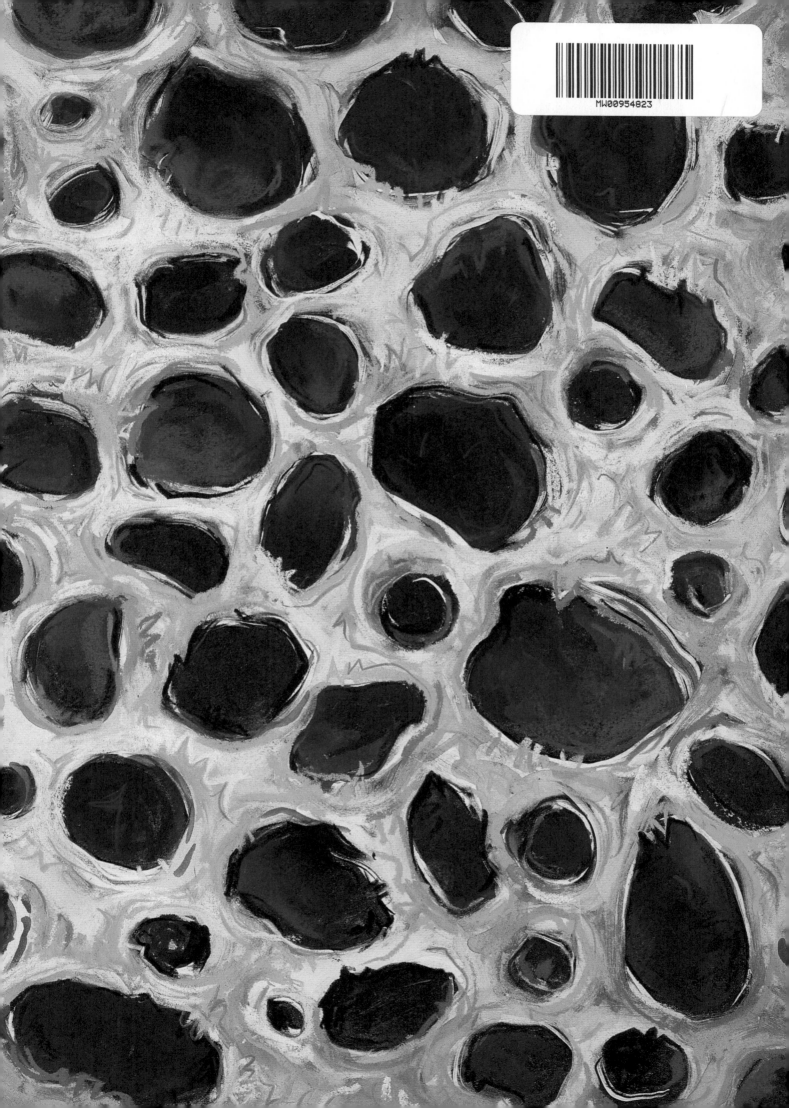

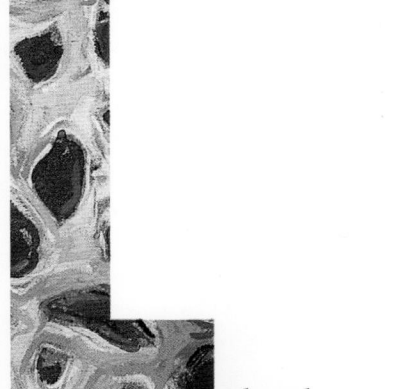a la salama.

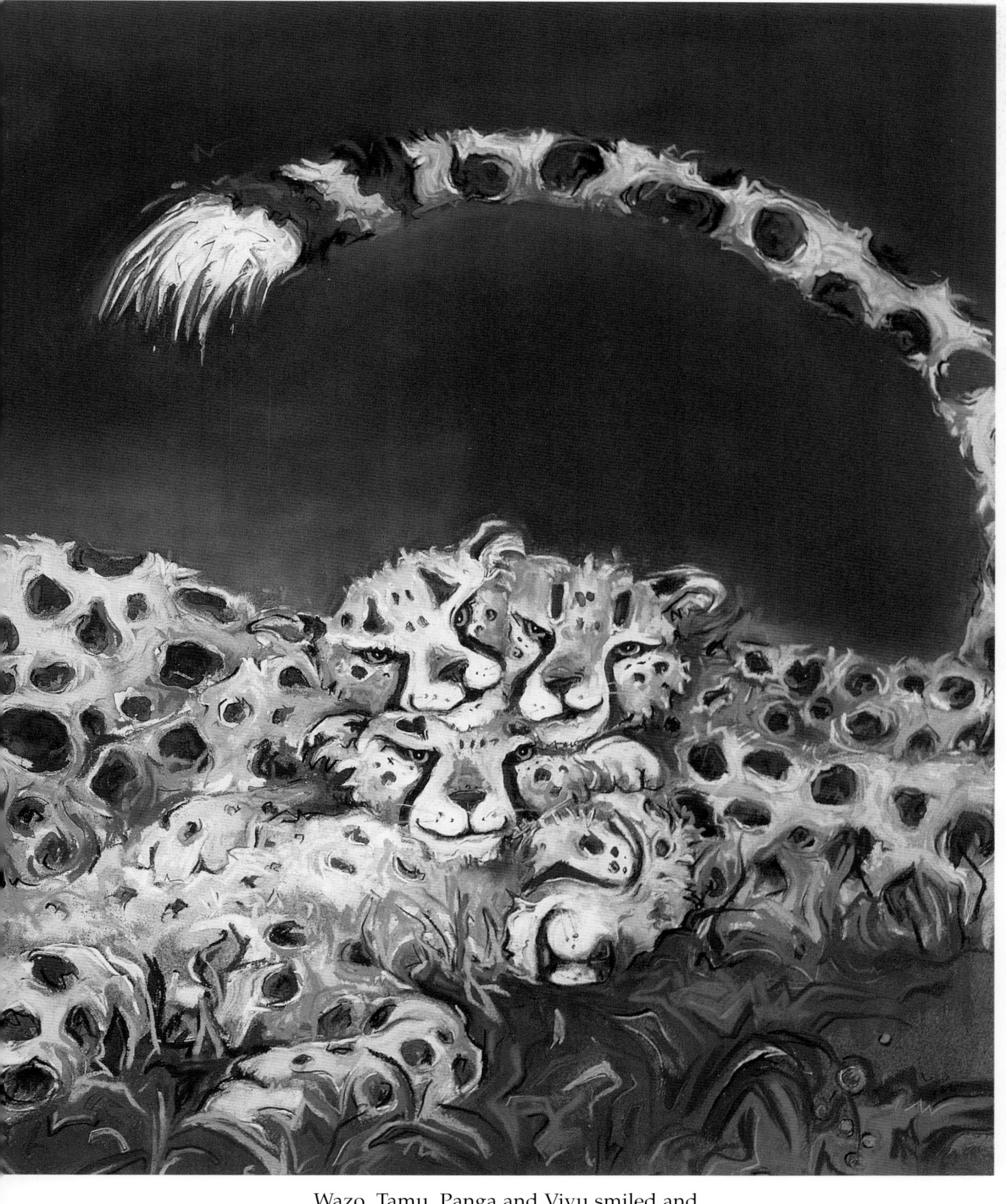

Wazo, Tamu, Panga and Vivu smiled and
purred. Mama Duma nuzzled each in turn.
After the meal, they curled up together
for the night.

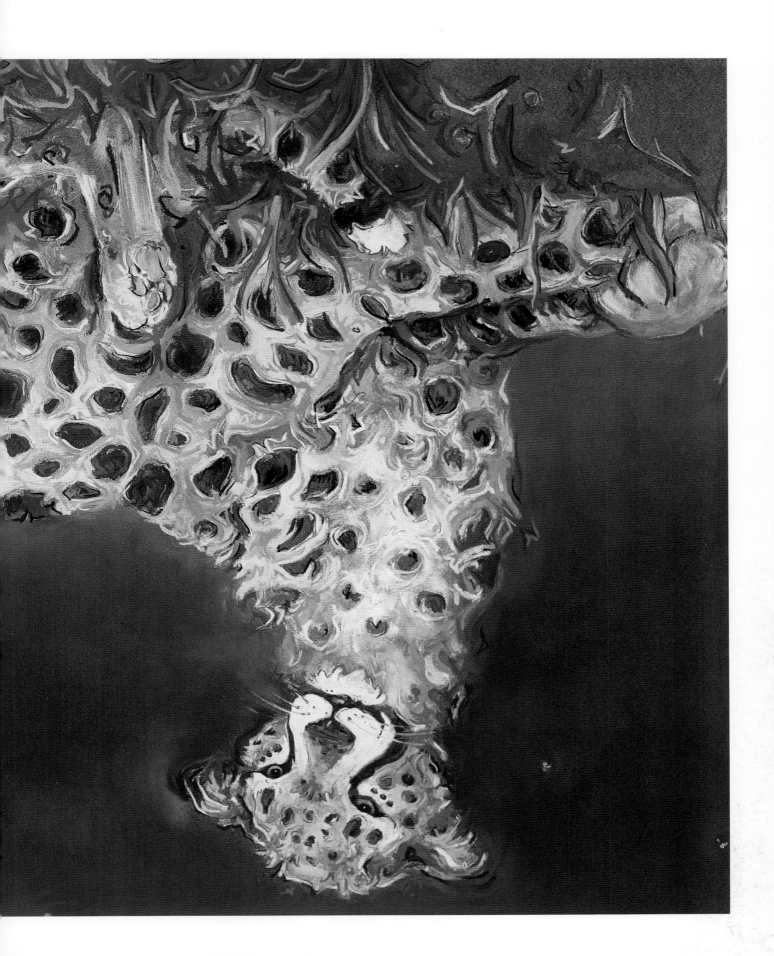

Punda Milia said, 'Your watoto were wise.
They act as cheetahs should.' "

Twiga said, 'Your watoto were respectful.
They are learning much.'

Mamba said, 'Your watoto were calm.
They cannot be tricked.'

Little Tembo said, 'Your watoto were cautious. They think before they act.'

Mbuni said, 'Your watoto were firm.
They will stand their ground.'

The light was fading. Mama Duma
returned with a feast for them all and a story
she heard as she hunted on the savanna.

"I met many animals today," she said.
"Ostriches, elephants, crocodiles, giraffes,
and zebras. They all spoke with awe and
respect about four little cheetahs. Were these
my four children, I wondered?

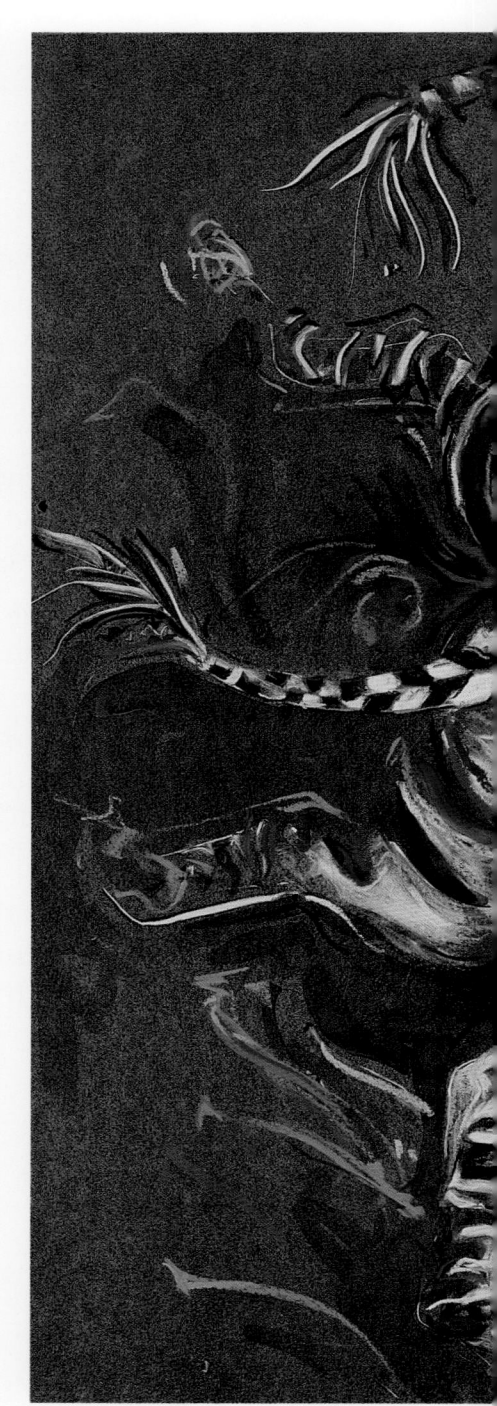

Suddenly, Wazo stuck out his tongue. "The air tastes of salt and dust. There are many animals coming our way, and quickly."

"What kind of animals?" asked Tamu.

But before Wazo could answer, several black and white faces were looking at the children through the grass.

"Jambo, watoto!" said a zebra in a voice as shrill as a wind storm. "My name is Punda Milia. My herd and I have run with the gnu, impala, and the strong oryx. We would like to race with you!"

But Panga said, "The day has grown long. It is time to wait, not to play."

"Asante sana," said Tamu. "You are beautiful and graceful. But I am content to watch you from here."

Wazo said, "We are cheetahs, the fastest animals on earth. We do not need to race you."

"We'll just stretch out here in the sun and rest," said Vivu. "Mother will be back soon."

With ears twitching and tails swishing, the zebras galloped off.

"How content they seem," Panga said.

"The zebras are happy being zebras," Tamu said.

"And how content we are," Vivu said.

"We are happy being cheetahs," Wazo said.

The day grew longer as the sun traveled to the west. The little cheetahs lay down and closed their eyes to rest. But Tamu felt the cool shadow of clouds fall over the spot where she lay. She opened one eye and looked at the sky. They were not clouds at all, but tall animals with long necks and gentle faces.

"Jambo, watoto!" said a giraffe in a voice as soft as a flamingo feather. "My name is Twiga. How can you see anything there, hiding in the grass? You should come up where we are and see the world. The plain stretches far and there is so much to be learned, so much to know."

Vivu opened his eyes.

Panga and Wazo did, too.

"In the treetops are secrets and in the distant mountains lie mysteries," said Twiga. "Will you come with us and see our world?"

"Yes," agreed the other giraffe. He tugged a leaf from the acacia tree and chewed it slowly. "We would enjoy your company."

But Tamu answered, "Asante sana. Your invitation is very kind. I see there is much you can share. But we are young cheetahs. We will stay here and learn about bugs and grasses and watering holes."

The giraffes smiled, nodded their great heads, and moved on.

"Tamu is right," said Vivu. "Cheetahs need to learn many things. For now, we must discover the little wonders around us and later we'll explore the bigger world beyond us."

The sun rose high, beating down on all below. Vivu frowned and his whiskers began to twitch. "I smell something rotten," he said. "Something cold and creepy." The other three lifted their noses and sniffed the air.

"What can it be?" asked Tamu.

There, floating like a log in the water, was a bumpy, scaly creature.

"Jambo, watoto!" said a crocodile in a voice as dry as rattling bones. "My name is Mamba. You've been waiting for your mother a long time, and she hasn't come back. Are you hungry? Won't you come join me for a tasty meal?"

Panga and Wazo began to shiver.

Tamu began to shake.

But Vivu, with a single leap, jumped onto a broken limb of the acacia tree and said, "Stay calm. Follow me."

They all scampered up the tree and watched until the crocodile, grumbling with disappointment, slithered out of sight.

Vivu said, "It does no good to lose your head."

"Vivu is right," said Wazo. "Cheetahs are calm when danger is around. This keeps us safe from harm."

"Shhh," said Wazo. "Do you hear that?"

The four furry heads tipped, listening. From beyond the grasses, they heard the sound of drums. "Boom, boom, boom!"

The four cheetahs sat without moving, squinting out through the thick grasses with wide eyes. The sound of drums came again, very close now, pounding the earth and making them tremble.

They held their breath. They closed their eyes.

Suddenly, Panga was hit between the ears with a spray of water. He hissed and rolled away, swiping at his fur with a front paw. It was then that a large gray head peeked through the grass and a large gray trunk sniffed the four children.

"Jambo, watoto!" said a baby elephant in a voice as strong as a granite stone. "My name is Little Tembo. I see you hiding there. Don't think I don't! Are you hot in the sun? Swim with my family! See them splashing? How cool and kind the water is, little cats. Come have a refreshing drink."

Vivu stood and stretched. "Floating in the water would be very pleasant. We can join Little Tembo for just a few minutes."

Tamu and Panga cheered, "Let's go!"

But two cheetah paws came down on two little tails and one set of teeth caught the third. Vivu, Tamu and Panga spun about to see Wazo, holding them tightly. "No," said Wazo. "Don't go into the water." And to Little Tembo she said, "We don't swim, but we'll watch your family swimming from our place in the grass."

Little Tembo patted each cheetah on the head with his trunk. Then he clambered down into the water. Soon the elephants climbed up the bank on the other side of the watering hole and vanished beyond the tussock grass.

"Wazo is right," sighed Panga. "Cheetahs are special. We can go for days without a drink. We don't need to leave the grass."

"Look!" said Wazo, her ears pricking up. "Do you see the grass rustling? Something is coming to our hiding place."

"It's nothing more than a breeze," said Panga. "You are always imagining things."

But then a huge, feathered creature appeared on the bank of the watering hole and spun around on big, floppy feet.

"Jambo, watoto!" said an ostrich in a voice as tickly as beetle legs. "My name is Mbuni. Won't you come spin with me? The day is warm and bright, just right for foolishness." He waved his giant wings and shook his fluffy tail and danced a wild, dizzy dance. Dust and flies were caught in the whirlwind of his spinning.

Tamu sneezed.

Vivu coughed.

But the ostrich did not stop. On and on he twirled, faster and faster, giggling as he went, until he lost his balance and fell, PLOP! into the watering hole.

"Oh, poor thing!" said Tamu.

"No!" said Panga. "He is a silly, careless thing! There are dangers in the water, some with sharp teeth and keen eyes!"

The little cheetahs watched as Mbuni climbed from the water and shook himself off. Panga pounced at him with a hiss and a yip, chasing him away.

"Panga is right," said Tamu. "Cheetahs can have fun, but we must be careful as we play." With that, she spun around to chase her own tail, and the others joined in the game.

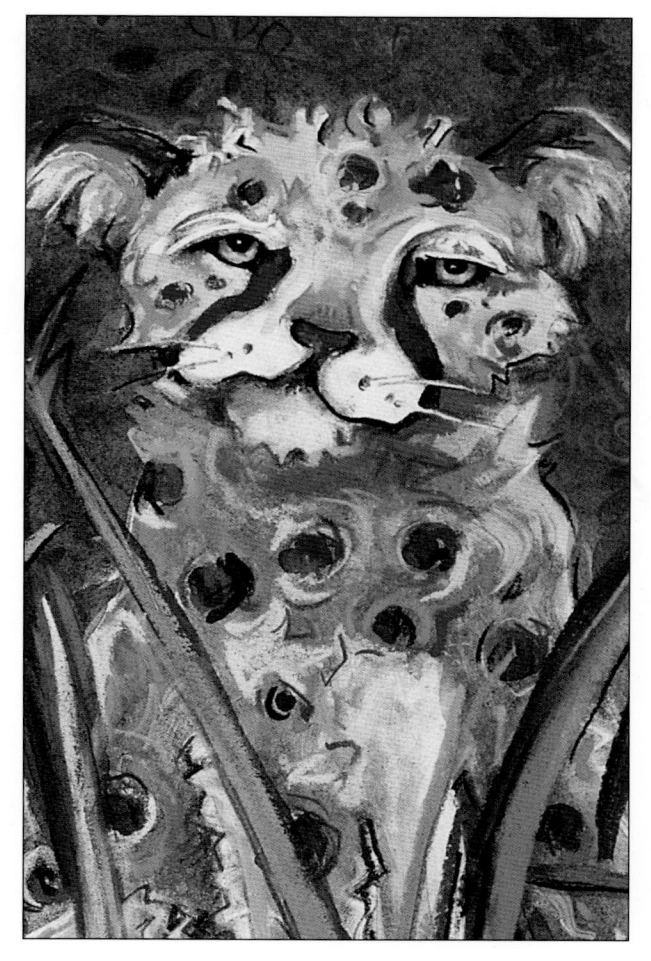

"The grass is soft and comfortable," said
lazy Vivu, in a voice as slow as a summer
afternoon. "Just right for a nap."

"Every day we must do the same thing,"
said grumpy Panga in a voice as dreary as
an endless savanna rain. "How boring."

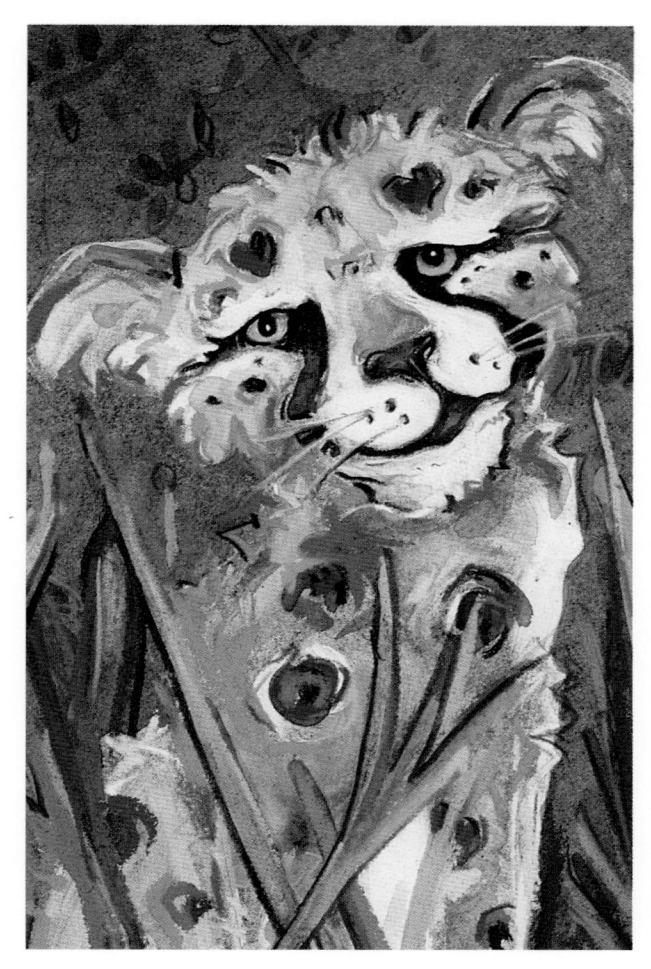

"This is such an interesting place," said
sweet Tamu in a voice as gentle as a
fig flower. "We can watch the butterflies
and dung beetles."

"We will wait here while mother is hunting,"
said bossy Wazo, in a voice as sharp
as a thorn bush. "That is how it must be."

Wazo, Tamu, Panga, and Vivu
listened until they could no longer hear
their mother's footsteps.

With a whisper of paw-step and a brush
of white-tipped tail, she was gone.

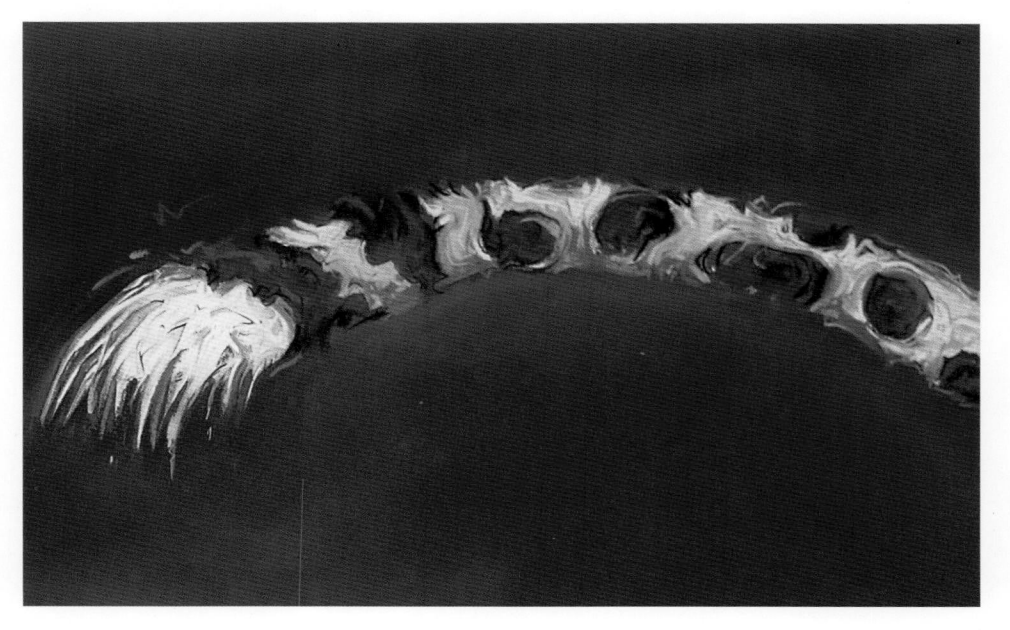

"Stay here, hidden in the grass in the shade
of this acacia tree by the watering hole.
I must go off to hunt. And soon, my watoto,
I will return with a fine meal for us all."

Stay, my watoto," said
Mama Duma. "Stay here and be safe."

For the cheetahs and other beasties
of East Africa. May they live forever wild.

Glossary — Swahili, a language of East Africa

Asante (ah-SAHN-teh) — **thank you**

Duma (DOO-mah) — **cheetah**

Jambo (JAHM-bo) — **hello**

La la salama (LAH LAH sah-LAH-mah) — **sleep in peace**

Mamba (MAHM-bah) — **crocodile**

Mbuni (m-BOO-ne) — **ostrich**

Panga (PAHN-gah) — **a large knife**

Punda milia (POON-dah me-LE-ah) — **zebra**

Sana (SAH-nah) — **very much**

Tamu (TAH-moo) — **sweet**

Tembo (TEHM-bo) — **elephant**

Twiga (TWE-gah) — **giraffe**

Vivu (VE-voo) — **lazy**

Watoto (wah-TO-to) — **children**

Wazo (WAH-zo) — **idea**

Jambo, Watoto!

Copyright © 1998 by Marsha Heatwole and
Creative Art Press
ISBN 0-9642712-3-0
Library of Congress Catalog Card Number 97-068117
Cataloging data for this book is available from the Library
of Congress.

Design: Carol Gerhardt
Printed in Hong Kong
First Edition, 1998

About the art

"The color pictures used in this book are done by a process
that I call altered monotype. First I do a sort of finger-
painting on plexi-glass with black etching ink. Then I trans-
fer the image to paper by rolling the plexi-glass and paper
together through an etching press. This is the monotype
(one print). I then add to this image by drawing and painting on the paper with chalk pastel, watercolor, gouache and
colored pencils."   M.H.

Jambo, Watoto!

By Marsha Heatwole

Text by Elizabeth Massie
and Barbara Spilman Lawson

Creative Art Press

West Bloomfield, Michigan

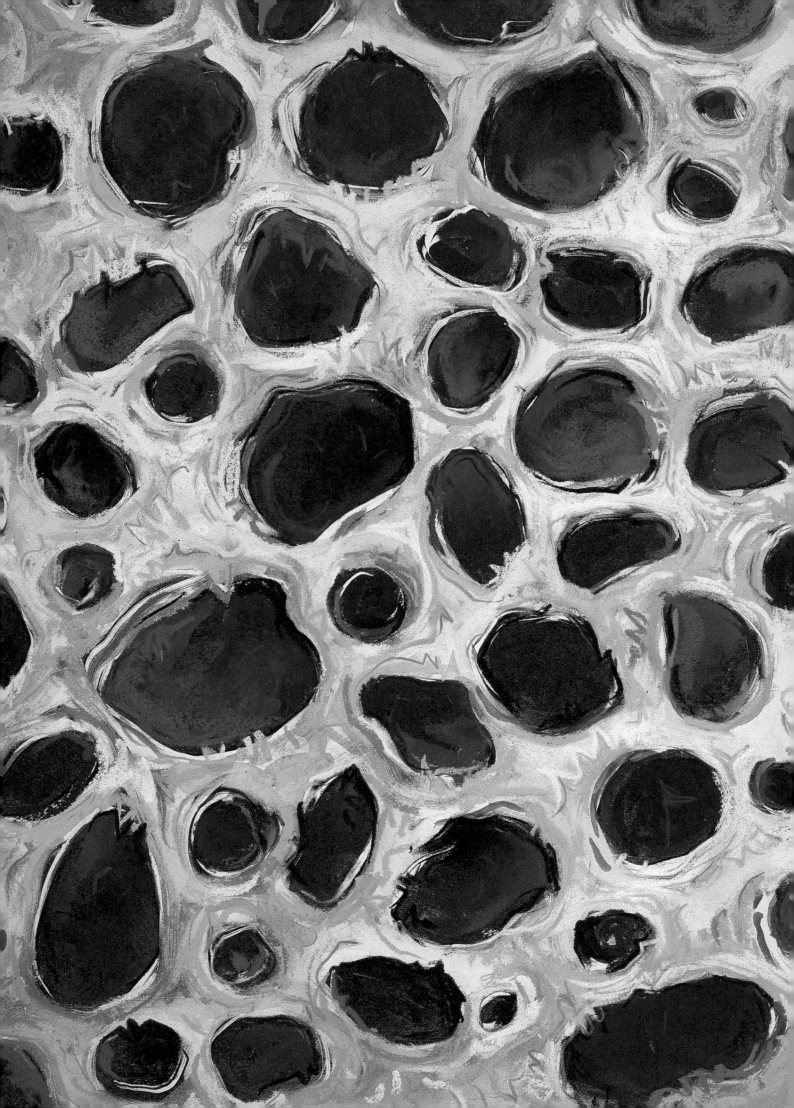